Multicultural Stories

from

China

by

Saviour Pirotta

Illustrated by Tim Clarey

WAYLAND

Series Editor: Paul Mason
Art Director: Jane Hawkins
Designer: Tessa Barwick

Printed in Malaysia

First published in 1999 by Wayland

This edition published in 2017 by Wayland,
an imprint of Hachette Children's Group

British Library Cataloguing in Publication Data
Pirotta, Saviour
Stories from China. – (Multicultural Stories)
1. Tales– China– Juvenile Literature
I. Title II Clarey, Tim
398.2'0951
ISBN-13: 9781526303721

Wayland
Carmelite House, 50 Victoria Embankment, London EC4Y 0DZ
Wayland is an imprint of Hachette Children's Group, an Hachette UK Company
www.hachette.co.uk
www.hachettechildrens.co.uk

Contents

Introduction

Like many other people my age, I first heard about China in school. The teachers told us some mind-boggling facts about it: China is the third largest country in the world - a quarter of the world's people live there; the Great Wall of China is so big, astronauts can see it from outer space.

Chinese people invented many things that are a vital part of modern life. They were the first to use coins and paper money. They made the first paper and discovered how to print long before anyone else. They also constructed the first compass and set off the first fireworks. Clearly the people of China were brilliant inventors; I have the greatest admiration for them.

Then, when I got interested in storytelling, I discovered another side to China, one that you never hear about during geography lessons. It is the China of myth and magic. Chinese people have an incredible wealth of folk tales and legends. They range from brilliant creation myths to simple fables that might help children understand a religious idea or a proverb. Then there are the stories about the festivals. They are full of monsters and fabulous, dangerous dragons.

Here are some stories that have become firm favourites of mine. I hope they'll be an exciting introduction to the world of Chinese stories.

Saviour

RUSSIA

YELLOW
SEA

MONGOLIA

NORTH
KOREA

SOUTH
KOREA

Beijing

Great Wall

Yellow River

C H I N A

Shanghai

EAST
CHINA SEA

H I M A L A Y A S

NEPAL

Yangzi River

INDIA

Guangzho

Hong Kong

C
H
I
N
A

BUTAN

MYANMAR

LAOS

VIETNAM

Hainan

THAILAND

SOUTH
CHINA SEA

China is such a large country that it shares its borders with many others, including India, Nepal,
Vietnam and Russia. The map on the top left shows China's position in the world.

STORIES OF HOW THE WORLD BEGAN

According to Chinese legend, the universe was created by a giant called Pan Gu. For 18,000 years, Pan Gu lay inside an egg which floated about in the darkness. Then one day the giant took an axe and smashed the egg to pieces. The light part of the egg floated up and became the sky. The heavy part sank and became the earth.

When Pan Gu died, his body turned into mountains. His blood became the rivers and the sea. His bones slowly changed into precious stones and minerals. Stars came out of his hair, while plants and trees emerged from his skin. Some say that Pan Gu's eyes became the sun and the moon. His breath was the wind.

Many years after Pan Gu's death, other gods and goddesses appeared. One of them was Nu Kua, the main character in our first story.

Mount Everest, on the border of China and Nepal, is the highest mountain in the world. We can only wonder which part of Pan Gu created this magnificent mountain.

The Legend of Nu Kua

For many years after Pan Gu's death, the world lay still and silent. The forests grew thick and green. The rivers wound their way over hills and across plains. The seas lay still as glass, reflecting the sun and the moon.

Then one day a goddess discovered the world. She was Nu Kua, half woman, half serpent. 'Oh what a beautiful place,' she gasped. 'Pan Gu was so clever to make it.' She sauntered through the forests, breathing in the smell of the flowers. She watched the animals and the birds, and teased the fish in the sea.

'What a pity I have no one to share Pan Gu's creation with,' thought Nu Kua. 'All these seas and countries are going to waste.' She scooped up some yellow mud and made a doll. 'There,' she said, setting the doll down on the ground, 'now I've got a friend.'

The doll trembled and opened its eyes. 'Hello,' said Nu Kua.

The doll, being a mortal, could not see or hear the goddess. 'Is anyone there?' it called. 'Am I alone?'

Nu Kua made more dolls. She put them down where they would find each other. The dolls soon learnt to live in the forest. They built huts and fires. They went hunting and fishing, and in the evening, they sang songs about the magic serpent-woman they saw in their dreams. Time passed and Nu Kua's dolls filled the land. They were the first people, and the goddess kept watch over them, to make sure they didn't get hurt or lonely or lost.

Now up in the heavens there were more gods. One of them was Gong Gong, the god of water. He was always quarrelling with Zhu Rong, the god of fire.

One day Gong Gong and Zhu Rong had a fight. They chased each other across the sky. Zhu Rong threw a flash of lightning at Gong Gong. Gong Gong hurled a typhoon which swept Gong Gong out of the heavens. The god of fire was livid. He shot a thunderbolt at his enemy and knocked him out of the sky. Zhu Rong was so angry he banged his head against one of the mountains holding up the heavens. The mountain crumbled, and a big part of the sky came crashing down on the world. The forests were flattened. The rivers flooded their banks. All over the world, thousands of volcanoes erupted, filling the sky with fire and lava.

Enormous cracks appeared in the ground and horrible beasts and monsters climbed out of them. They started gobbling up the people, who tried to hide in deep caves. It seemed Pan Gu's beautiful world had come to an end.

Nu Kua could not bear the havoc. Quickly, she melted some stones to make special glue. Soon she had patched up the sky.

Then she looked for something to hold up the heavens. The four mountains were gone. So Nu Kua found a giant turtle that had died in the floods and used its legs as pillars. Then she blew out the volcanoes.

The monsters did not like that. They howled and bashed their tails against the ground. Nu Kua was not scared. She snatched an evil dragon in her right hand and flung it far out into the sky. That scared the monsters. They ran back into their holes and hid there in the dark. Nu Kua stopped up the holes with earth, so they could not come out again and eat the people.

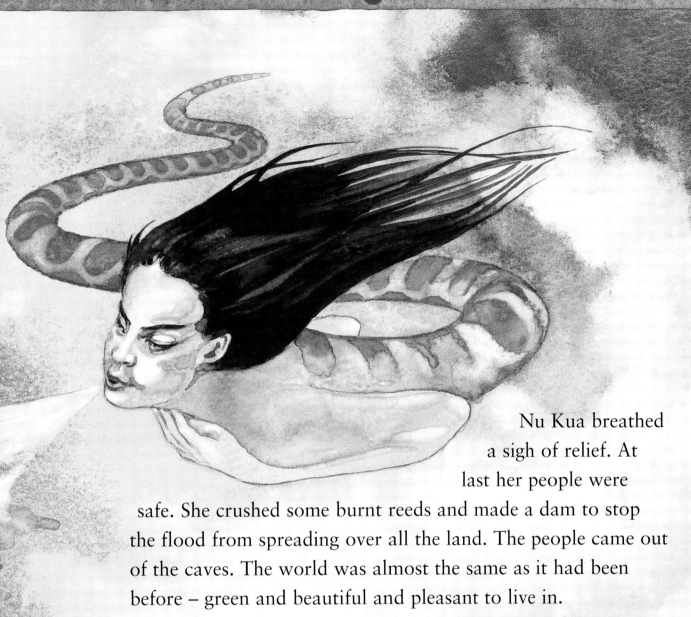

Nu Kua breathed
a sigh of relief. At
last her people were
safe. She crushed some burnt reeds and made a dam to stop
the flood from spreading over all the land. The people came out
of the caves. The world was almost the same as it had been
before – green and beautiful and pleasant to live in.

'I shall never let anyone hurt you again,' promised Nu Kua,
retreating into the skies where she could keep watch on Gong
Gong and Zhu Gong.

Time passed and Nu Kua's people spread to every country in
the world. They learned to work and cook, and to write stories
telling about their life on earth. In time they invented machines
and built huge cities. No one remembered Nu Kua anymore.
But sometimes they looked up at the sky and wondered if there
was anyone out there, watching over them, making sure they
didn't get hurt or lonely or lost.

CHINESE DRAGONS

The dragons of Chinese legend are not monsters. They are gods who bring much-needed rain to the people. The ancient Chinese believed that dragons made rain clouds with their breath. Most dragons went to sleep in winter. Then the land became dry and arid. But in spring the dragons woke up. As they emerged from their caves, the rains returned to water the earth.

Children who found large pebbles on the riverbank often thought they were dragon's eggs. They never touched them, for they believed that when there were thunderstorms, the eggs would crack open and baby dragons would fly out of them.

When dragons fought, they caused floods and thunderstorms. Sometimes they also dropped pearls on the ground. It was considered lucky to find a dragon's pearl; it meant you were going to find water, a lot of water.

China has two main rivers: the Yangzi River and the Yellow River. Who knows how many dragon's eggs might be lying on the riverbanks, just waiting to hatch?

The Dragon's Pearl

They say Xiao Sheng lived with his mother in a little town. Every morning he cut the wild grass outside his house. His mother sold it at the market and, on her way home, she bought rice and tea, and flour for dumplings.

One summer there was a terrible drought. All the grass outside Xiao's house wilted and died.

'Whatever shall we do?' said his mother. 'The rice jar is almost empty.'

'Don't worry, mother,' said Xiao. 'I'll find some grass for you to sell.' He put on his boots and trudged out to the forest. All day long he looked for a patch of grass. But the summer heat seemed to have killed everything. There was not a blade of green grass to be had anywhere. Xiao went back home.

'Have you found any grass?' asked his mother.

'No,' said Xiao sadly.

'I have,' said his mother. She held out a basket of freshly cut grass.

'Mother,' gasped Xiao. 'Where did you find that?'

'Behind the barn,' said his mother. She led Xiao to the spot where she'd picked the grass. 'There, look. It's grown again. You can't even tell I cut it this morning.'

Xiao knelt on the hard, dry ground. He poked his finger in the grass. There was something caught in the roots. Xiao dug it up.

'It's a precious pearl,' said his mother.

'A dragon's pearl,' whispered Xiao. 'Its magic made the grass grow.'

'Let's hide it in the rice jar,' said his mother.

They hurried indoors and dropped the pearl in the jar. Xiao washed the grass in a wooden tub, ready for the market the next day, while his mother made supper with the last of the rice.

The next morning, Ma shook Xiao awake. 'Look, son,' she gasped. 'The rice jar is full.' Xiao stared at the jar. Ma was right. It was filled right up to the brim with rice. 'It's the dragon's pearl again,' said Ma. She poured some rice in her apron and took it next door to the neighbours. 'You must share in our good fortune,' she said. The neighbours were delighted. They told their friends about the pearl and the rice. Soon there was a crowd outside Xiao's cottage. Ma gave some rice to everyone.

News of the dragon's pearl spread to other villages. People came from far and wide to see the pearl in the jar and to get some rice. Xiao and his mother made everyone welcome.

Alas, kindness is not always repaid with gratitude. Some people got jealous of Xiao and his mother. They wanted the pearl for themselves.

'Let's break into Xiao's house and steal it,' said a man.

'Yes,' said his friend. 'Then we could charge people for the rice.'

At night the men broke into Xiao's house. They looked around in the dark, trying to find the rice jar.

'Who's there?' called Xiao's mother, waking up. She leapt out of bed and dashed into the kitchen. The men rushed at her with clubs. 'Give us the pearl,' they said.

'Never,' said Xiao's ma.

Xiao came into the kitchen, rubbing the sleep from his eyes.

'Quick, son,' said his mother. 'Get the pearl from the water bucket.' The burglars dived at the bucket. Xiao chuckled. His mother was a clever one. He flew at the rice jar and fished out the pearl.

'Hey,' said the burglars, 'hand that over.'

'Never,' said Xiao. He popped the pearl in his mouth and swallowed it.

'Son!' Ma screamed.

Xiao felt a searing pain in his stomach. He fell to his knees, trembling. 'Son,' cried his ma. 'Dragon's pearls are poisonous.' Xiao looked at her through a veil of tears. The fire in his belly was spreading to his feet and hands. It was reaching inside his head, drying up his mouth. He looked at his hands: his skin was turning green and scaly.

'Ma,' he whispered,
'I am changing into a dragon.'

His mother led him outside, wailing. He fell to the
ground and closed his eyes. The pain was eating him up,
like salt eats into a helpless snail. He thought he could
hear voices calling, and music, and crashes of thunder.

Then there was silence.

He opened his eyes again. The pain was gone. The
colours around him were bright and vivid. The sky was
clear. He looked down: he was no longer on the ground;
he was high up in the air, beating dragon wings,
breathing dragon fire.

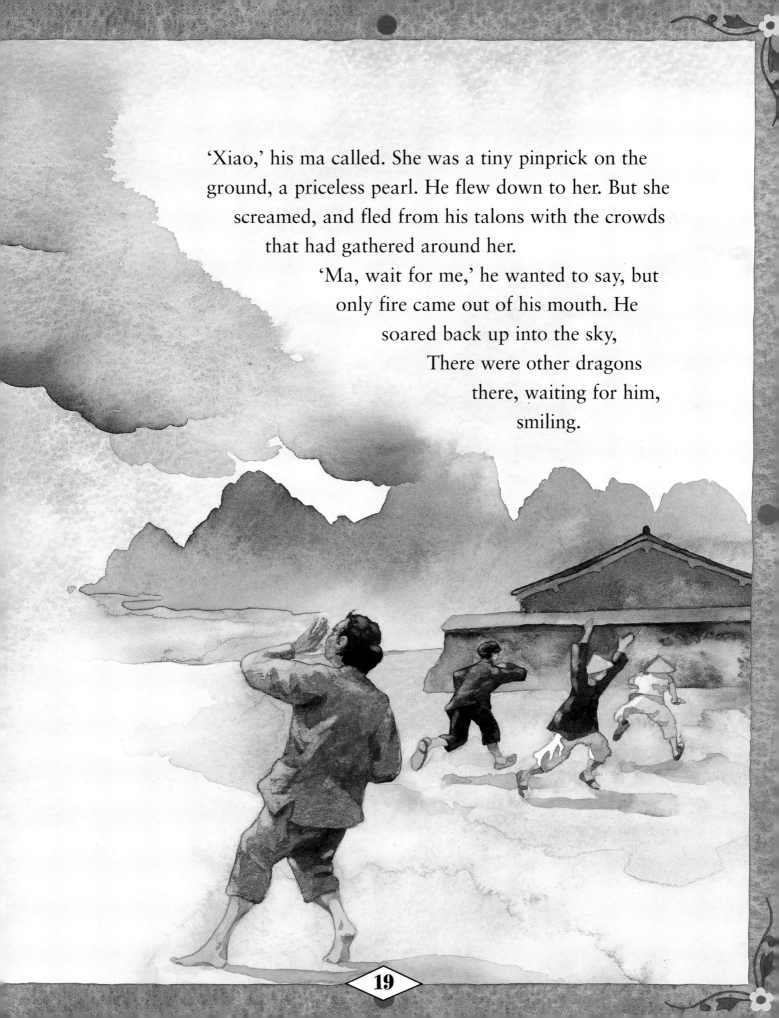

'Xiao,' his ma called. She was a tiny pinprick on the ground, a priceless pearl. He flew down to her. But she screamed, and fled from his talons with the crowds that had gathered around her.

'Ma, wait for me,' he wanted to say, but only fire came out of his mouth. He soared back up into the sky, There were other dragons there, waiting for him, smiling.

'Dance,' they said, 'dance, for you are now a water dragon.'

He danced, tears of loneliness dripping from his eyes. His wings churned up the sky, making clouds.

It started to rain.

Down below, the grass would be turning green, he thought. But he'd never pick grass again, never talk to his ma again.

The crowds, standing in the rain, cheered and danced. 'Your son has saved us all,' they said to his ma. 'We are grateful.'

Tired, the water dragon settled on the swelling river.

'Come with us,' said the other dragons. 'A new world awaits you.'

Xiao-Dragon followed his new friends, but every now and then he turned, hoping to catch one last glimpse of his ma in the crowds. He tried waving, but every time he turned to wave, his wings cut into the river bank. Twenty-eight times the dragon turned to wave to Ma, and always his wings caught in the bank.

'Goodbye, Ma,' he called. 'Goodbye, my little pearl.'

Soon he'd disappeared altogether. There was nothing left to show that Old Ma had once had a wonderful son, nothing but twenty-eight twists in the river leading to the little town.

☷ ZODIAC ☷ MONKEYS

The Chinese calendar is divided into a twelve-year cycle. Each year is symbolised by an animal. There are years dedicated to the Rat, the Ox, the Tiger, the Dragon, the Snake, the Horse, the Sheep, the Monkey, the Rooster, the Dog and the Pig.

Ancient priests used to say that people inherit the characteristics of the animal that symbolises the year they were born in. So people born in the Year of the Tiger are meant to be fearless and aggressive, while those born in the Year of the Ox are believed to be strong, patient and quiet.

People born in the Year of the Monkey are regarded as curious, mischievous and successful. But how many of these are truly the characteristics of the monkey? Read on.

The Yunnan snub-nosed monkey is one of the rarest monkeys in the world. Their main population of 1,500 lives in southern China's Yung Ling mountains.

Monkeys in Hats

The farmer set off to the city. It was market day and he had some grass hats to sell. When the sun rose he stopped to eat his breakfast under a tree. 'It's still early' he said to himself. 'I think I'll have a little snooze.'

The farmer put on a hat. Then he lay back on the grass and closed his eyes. The morning sun got brighter and stronger. Its rays reached through the branches of the trees, making him sweat. 'I need another hat over my face,' thought the farmer. He reached into the basket. But there were no hats there. They were all gone.

The farmer sat bolt upright. His jaw dropped open. He looked around him, expecting to see thieves hiding behind the tree trunk. But he was alone.

'Hey,' shouted the farmer to no one in particular, 'give me back my hats, whoever you are.'

There was a snigger in the branches overhead. The farmer looked up. The tree was full of monkeys, each one wearing one of his hats. 'You give me back those hats,' yelled the farmer.

The monkeys laughed and scratched their bottoms. 'Yooo, yooo, yoo,' they shouted back.

'I'm coming to get you,' said the farmer. He climbed up the tree, huffing and puffing. The monkeys watched him with a merry twinkle in their eye. Then, just as he reached the first branch, they all leapt nimbly to the ground.

'Yeee, yeee, yeee,' they laughed, sticking their tongues out at him.

The farmer jumped down and chased the monkeys across the grass. But it was no use. They were too fast for him.

At last the farmer sat down under the tree, defeated. The monkeys gathered in the branches above him, watching him closely.

The farmer fanned his face with his hat. Immediately, all the monkeys fanned their faces too.

The farmer scratched his chin.

So did the monkeys!

That gave the farmer an idea. He stood up slowly. Then he threw his hat into the basket.

The monkeys all did the same.

'Gotcha,' cried the farmer. And he snapped the basket lid shut.

The monkeys gibbered and screeched but there was nothing they could do. They'd been tricked. Which goes to prove that a silly monkey will always be silly, no matter what kind of hat it wears.

LEGENDARY MONSTERS

Chinese folklore is full of beasts and monsters. One of the fiercest is the Hai Ho Shang, a monster fish with a shaved head that lived in the South China Sea. Fishermen say it used to drag ships down to the murky depths.

Another ancient beast was the Gigantopithecus. A huge primate, half man, half ape, it was believed to have become extinct 300,000 years ago. But people from Central and Southern China still report sightings of an elusive beast. It looks like a giant ape but has a snout and human eyes. They call it The Yeren. People travelling after dark keep a sharp look out for it.

Still, it seems the beast to avoid is not the Yeren. It is the one you can read about in our next story.

The South China Sea is certainly deep enough for a large beast to hide in its waters. Its maximum depth is 5,015 m.

The Fiercest Beast

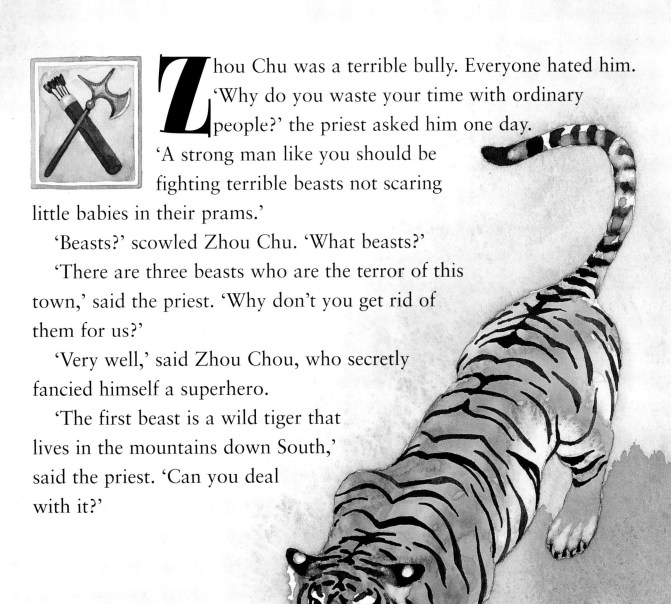

Zhou Chu was a terrible bully. Everyone hated him. 'Why do you waste your time with ordinary people?' the priest asked him one day. 'A strong man like you should be fighting terrible beasts not scaring little babies in their prams.'

'Beasts?' scowled Zhou Chu. 'What beasts?'

'There are three beasts who are the terror of this town,' said the priest. 'Why don't you get rid of them for us?'

'Very well,' said Zhou Chou, who secretly fancied himself a superhero.

'The first beast is a wild tiger that lives in the mountains down South,' said the priest. 'Can you deal with it?'

'You just watch me,' said Zhou Chou, flexing his muscles.

He took his axe and his arrows, and he hurried up into the mountains. There he found the tiger sharpening its teeth on a dead tree trunk. Zhou Chou hurled his axe at it, then he shot his arrows. The tiger dodged them but Zhou leapt at it and crushed its skull with his bare hands.

'Well done,' said the priest when he returned home with the tiger skin. 'Now you must conquer the second beast – a water dragon.'

Zhou Chou took a boat and ventured out on to the river. The water dragon came at him from the front. Then it came at him from the back. Zhou Chou stuck his tongue out at it. When it came close to set him on fire, he stuck his axe between its eyes.

'You are indeed a hero,' said the priest when Zhou Chou returned home wearing a necklace of dragon teeth. 'Now you must conquer the fiercest beast of all.'

'Tell me where I can find the wretch,' boasted Zhou Chou, brandishing his axe.

'He is standing right in front of me,' said the priest. 'You are the fiercest beast, Zhou Chou.'

The bully's mouth dropped open. For the first time in his life, he felt small and ashamed of himself. He realized that his bullying had made him a much bigger monster than the wild tiger and the water dragon.

So from then on he was nice to everyone he met.

CHINESE NEW YEAR

The Chinese celebrate the arrival of the Chinese New Year with a big festival. A few days before New Year's Eve, people clean their houses to clear out bad luck and misfortune. Some paint their doors and windows red. Decorations are hung in every room, window and doorway.

On New Year's Eve, families gather to have a feast. They eat a lot of food, including boiled dumplings. At midnight they watch fireworks and burn firecrackers. The lights are kept on all night to welcome in the New Year.

On New Year's Day, children receive packets of lucky money. Then they visit friends and relatives to exchange gifts. The celebrations continue for two weeks. People buy special flowers, go to fairs and watch the special Lion Dance, which brings good luck to all who see it.

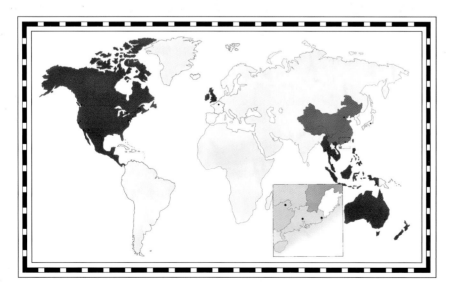

Chinese New Year is also celebrated outside China. █ *The areas in red show where many Chinese people live today.*

The Lion Dance

 The Nien was a terrible monster. It had sharp teeth and big claws and when it roared, even the moon seemed to tremble. No one was safe from the Nien. It liked eating babies and grannies and, most of all, it liked gobbling up children on their way back home from school.

One evening, towards the end of the year, some people gathered in a tavern. They'd met to make plans for the New Year festival.

'Let's have a really big celebration this year,' said a farmer.

'Yes,' said his friends, 'let's have lanterns and music, and lots of food.'

Soon everyone in the village was busy getting ready for the festival. The children cleaned out their rooms to sweep away the bad luck, while the grown-ups painted the windows bright red to attract good fortune.

Everything seemed to be going well until, just a few days before the festival, an old cobbler burst into the tavern.

'The Nien's been seen outside the village,' he gasped. 'They say he's gobbled up a farmer and three geese.'

'What shall we do?' wondered the villagers. 'We can't have a festival while the Nien is about. He might eat up some of the children.'

'We could ask the fox to chase it away,' said a farmer. 'Foxes are very good at chasing things.'

So the villagers asked the fox to deal with the Nien. The fox was very brave. It chased the Nien right into the middle of the forest. But the fox never came back. The Nien had it for its supper.

The next day the villagers hired a tiger. Tigers are powerful creatures. The villagers thought theirs would make mincemeat of the Nien. But it didn't. The Nien chased it into a cave where it sat whimpering, trembling from head to toe like a coward.

So, in despair, the villagers called a lion. The lion was a bit long in the tooth but it was not afraid of the Nien. It howled and chased the monster round the countryside. The Nien tried to fight back. But the lion was too fast for it. The Nien could not harm it. In the end, it had to go and find its dinner somewhere else, away from the village.

'The monster's gone at last,' said a traveller who'd just come to the village across the plains. 'Some road builders saw it crossing the bridge by the mountains.'

'It is safe to have a party, then,' cheered the people. They brought out the food and put candles in the lanterns. They danced and played and, when the moon rose high in the sky, they set off their fireworks.

'Good riddance to the Nien,' they cried. 'Happy New Year.'

The year passed quickly and soon the villagers were busy once again preparing for the New Year celebrations.

'You won't believe this,' said an old woodcutter in the tavern, 'but that old Nien is back.'

'Never mind,' said his friends. 'We'll get the lion to chase it away again.' Two men went to see the lion.

'I'm afraid I can't make it this year,' said the mighty beast. 'The emperor has ordered me to stand guard outside his palace. I daren't leave my post.'

'What shall we do now?' wondered the villagers. 'No one but the lion can deal with the Nien.'

One of the men had an idea. 'I know what we can do,' he said. And he bent down and whispered his idea to his friends. Everyone set to work at once. They fetched canes and paper and pots of glue. The local artist washed his brushes. His assistant ground the paints: orange and yellow and bright bright black.

On New Year's Eve, the Nien crept to the village. It sniffed the air but it could not smell the lion. All it could smell was kids. Nice, juicy kids washed clean with soap. The Nien licked its lips. Soon it was going to have a feast. A really big feast.

The Nien bounded to the village square – only to find it empty. 'Funny,' thought the Nien, 'the little darlings should be out on the streets by now, dancing themselves silly. Where is everybody?'

Suddenly, a big, hulking shape leapt out of the dark. It was a horrible lion, twice as big as the one that had so humiliated the Nien the year before. The Nien jumped. The lion started dancing around it, its horrible eyes glowing like nasty little moons.

'You keep away from me,' roared the Nien, backing off down the street. 'You keep away from me or I'll tear you to shreds.'

The lion snickered and came closer, baring its enormous teeth. The poor Nien fled for its life.

'Hooray, we chased the Nien away,' cheered the children who'd been watching from behind the shutters in their windows.

The lion continued dancing down the street. People came out to dance around it. Soon the whole village was celebrating the beginning of a New Year.

After the party, the lion's head was packed away in a barn. It was only a huge mask, you see. The villagers had made a lion out of cane and paper, and three men had climbed inside it to make it move. The foolish Nien had been fooled.

Ever since then, Chinese people have had a lion dance every New Year. It keeps the evil Nien away for yet another year.

HOPPING GHOSTS

Chinese people always make sure that their dear departed have a decent burial. Dead people who are unhappy with their last resting place become ghosts. Their soul, called the Po, refuses to leave the world. It turns into an evil spirit.

Some people, especially those who are buried far from their village, become Hopping Ghosts. They dig their way out of the grave and try to make it back home. Only, the corpse becomes stiff with time. The legs refuse to bend. So the ghost has to hop.

Hopping ghosts are horrible. Some have eyes that keep falling out of the sockets. Others have black, swollen tongues that hang down to their chests. Worst of all, they have long, sharpened fingernails to cut up people with. So it's easy to spot a Hopping Ghost coming your way. Or is it? In the world of ghosts, nothing is ever what it seems.

Shanghai, where this story takes place, is one of China's largest cities. Over 13 million people live there.

This Hospital is Haunted

The children sat around in their ward, in Shanghai's main hospital, listening to the wind howling outside the window. There was Yi, and Chan, and the twins who both had a broken leg. It was a cold night. Yi shivered.

'They say this hospital is haunted,' said Chan, a girl who'd injured her back doing gymnastics.

'Haunted?' The twins looked around them in alarm. 'Haunted by what?'

'A hopping ghost,' said Chan. 'The orderly told me.'

A boy in the far corner coughed. 'The orderly doesn't know anything about ghosts,' he said.

'Pardon?' said Yi politely.

'The orderly,' repeated the boy with some difficulty, 'he knows nothing about ghosts.'

Chan noticed he had bandages around his face. 'The nurses must have moved him in here while we were having dinner,' she thought. 'No one saw him arrive, not even the twins who were always looking out of the window. Perhaps he'd been in intensive care, or in one of the adult wards. The nurses often put children there were they were short of space in the children's ward.'

'Do you know anything about ghosts?' asked Yi.

'Not much,' said the boy. He moved around on the bed, trying to get comfortable.

'Well, I do,' said Chan. 'The orderly told me that there is a ghost here. A horrible one.'

The twins gawped in unison. 'How horrible?' they wanted to know.

'Really horrible,' said Chan. 'It's the ghost of a thief. He broke in here one night, wanting to steal food from the kitchen. Cook heard him rustling around in the rice sacks. She called the police. And the orderly. That's how he knows.'

'Well...' began Yi.

'No...' said the boy in the bandages.

'Yes,' continued Chan, not giving anyone a chance to say their bit. 'Cook locked the thief in the kitchen. The wretch banged on the door with his fists. Cook said he swore like a trooper. Obviously, he'd been used to a life of crime.'

'But...' insisted the boy in the bandages.

Chan took no notice of him. She could see that the twins were under her spell now. Their eyes were as wide as saucers.

'The police got here at last,' she continued. 'They wanted to take the thief down to the police station. But he gave them the slip. He ran all around the wards, waking up the patients. One of the officers shouted at him. But it's useless shouting at thieves. He overturned some of the bedside cabinets, and some of the potties under the beds. There was pee everywhere.'

'Cook said the thief snatched a purse from a patient. He hadn't managed to steal food but he'd got some cash. He was over the moon. Apparently he waved the purse around so the police could see it.'

'Cor,' said one the twins.

'Cor,' repeated the other.

'No respect for the law,' said Yi.

'No respect,' echoed the boy in the bandages, managing to sit up.

'Of course, he never got away,' Chan went on. 'The police cornered him. So he jumped out of a window. He thought there was soft grass underneath or maybe a pond. But there were only rocks. The orderly says he was as limp as a string puppet when they brought him in. He died soon after and became a hopping ghost. I guess it's the money that keeps him here. You see, he let go of the purse before he jumped out of the window. The money went everywhere. He still wanders around at night, looking for coins under the beds.'

'That's not true,' spluttered the boy in the bandages, almost falling out of the bed in his effort to speak. 'I know that story and it's not like that. The guy wasn't a thief. He was a young monk, from the mountains. He and his mum had come all the way to the city to find his father. But the monk's mum got sick on the way. She had coughing fits and he was worried about her. So when they passed the hospital, he came in to see if the doctors would help her. Someone thought he was a worker here and sent him to the kitchen to fetch a bowl of rice. The cook made a mistake, and so did the orderly. And when the police came, it wasn't a purse he was waving around, it was an envelope. Inside it was a letter from the priest at his temple, saying he was studying to be a monk. Only the police never gave him a chance to show it to them. And then he slipped on the pee. He fell out of the open window. It was very tragic.'

'That's not what the orderly said,' argued Chan.

'You shouldn't believe everything you are told,' said the boy.

'How do you know all this?' asked Yi.

The boy managed to shuffle to his feet. You could tell there was something wrong with his bones. He was all stiff. 'I knew the monk myself,' he said. 'And he didn't come back for the money, he came back for the letter that said he was a student at the temple. That was very important to him.'

Slowly, painfully, he bent down and retrieved something from under the bed. 'There,' he whispered.

The others watched him hop across the room to the window. 'Goodbye,' he said, and next moment he was gone, leaving just a pile of soiled bandages on the floor for the orderly to clean up.

Glossary

Arid Very dry.

Dragons Mythical, winged, reptile-like monsters that breathe fire.

Dumplings Cases of flour containing pieces of meat and vegetables, which are fried or boiled.

Firecrackers Small cardboard containers filled with explosive powder. When lit, each one gives a loud bang.

Great Wall of China This ancient wall, built in 200 BC, runs for over 2,400 km across part of North China.

Lucky money Packets of money in red envelopes, with a good luck symbol on each packet, which are given to friends and relatives on New Year's Eve. Chinese people believe that red is a lucky colour.

Minerals Substances formed naturally in the earth, such as coal and iron.

Primate One of the most intelligent kinds of animals, including apes, monkeys and humans.

Proverb A popular truth or belief that is in the form of a short, memorable sentence.

Soul The spiritual part of a body believed to survive after death.

Typhoon A violent storm of wind and rain, especially in the seas of China.

Further Information

BOOKS:

The Legend Of The Chinese Zodiac – Susan Whitfield –
   Barefoot Books, 1997

Wishbones – Barbara Kerr Wilson – Frances Lincoln, 2007

The following books include some good stories from China:

The Illustrated Book of Myths – Neil Philip – Dorling Kindersely 1995, includes a detailed study of the Pan Gu legend.

The Orchard Book of Starry Tales – Geraldine McMaughrean – Orchard Books, 1998, has a fantastic story called 'The Bridge of Magpies'.

The Orchard Book of Mythical Birds and Beasts – Margaret Mayo – Orchard Books 1996, includes a wonderful flood myth that also features a dragon, called 'The Fish At Dragon's Gate'.

Some good information books on China:

C is for China by Sunwan So (Frances Lincoln, 2004)

Country Insights: China by Julia Waterlow (Hodder Wayland, 2006)

Festivals and Food: China by A. Shui and S. Thompson (Hodder Wayland, 2006)

The Changing Face of China by Stephen Keeler (Hodder Wayland, 2002)

China Activities

Turn the **Legend of Na Kua** into a play, imagining the conversations between Na Kua's dolls as they explored their surroundings. Write about their terror when they saw the monsters and their relief at being saved.

Trickster tales such as **Monkeys in Hats** and **The Fiercest Beast** always involve someone being tricked. Think of your own trickster tale involving a clever animal outwitting a person. Or, as in **The Fiercest Beast**, think how you could turn events around so a liar, cheat or bully has his or her actions thrown back at him or her.

In **The Dragon's Pearl**, Xiao is transformed into a water dragon. Write a story carrying on from where this story ends. Think about how lonely Xiao feels when he leaves his friends and mother behind. Then think about how he finds life as a dragon. Does he make friends with the other dragons? Does he enjoy flying over the country and what does he discover on his travels?

Chinese New Year is very colourful and lively, expecially the Chinese dragon costumes that weave through the streets. Design your very own Chinese dragon for the celebrations. It must look fierce to scare the terrible Nien in **The Lion Dance** story.

In **This Hospital is Haunted**, the children hear about the terrible ghost from the orderly's stories. Do you believe the ghost's side of the story? Write an article for the hospital's weekly newsletter revealing what you think the ghost's true story really is.